EGMONT

We bring stories to life

This edition published in Great Britain 2010 by Dean,
an imprint of Egmont UK Limited
239 Kensington High Street, London W8 6SA
All Rights Reserved

Thomas the Tank Engine & Friends™

CREATED BY BRITT ALLCROFT
Based on the Railway Series by the Reverend W Awdry
© 2010 Gullane (Thomas) LLC. A HIT Entertainment company.
Thomas the Tank Engine & Friends and Thomas & Friends are trademarks of Gullane (Thomas) Limited.
Thomas the Tank Engine & Friends and Design is Reg. U.S. Pat. & Tm. Off.

HiT entertainment

ISBN 978 0 6035 6415 4
5 7 9 10 8 6 4
Printed in Malaysia

Thomas'
Busy Day

It was a busy night on the Island
of Sodor and Thomas was trying
hard to be a Really Useful Engine.

Thomas' job was to deliver coal
to all the station waiting rooms.
He didn't want the passengers
to get cold.

Thomas knew he had a very important job to do and worked hard all night, steaming quickly along the tracks and through the icy countryside.

When Thomas' work was finally
done, he chuffed slowly into the
Engine Sheds, looking tired.

"I'm all puffed out," Thomas said.
"I wish I'd had some help today."

"Pah!" huffed Gordon. "A Really Useful Engine doesn't need help."

Thomas was cross, he wanted to show Gordon that he was a Really Useful Engine too.

Just then, The Fat Controller
arrived at the Sheds. "I need an
engine to run three specials
for me," he said.

"I can do it," puffed Thomas.
He was tired, but he knew this was
his chance to prove to Gordon that
he WAS a Really Useful Engine.

"Very well, Thomas," said The Fat Controller. "You must take some chickens to the market, the sheep to the farm and the children to school."

"That's a very big job for a small engine," whistled Gordon. "You're bound to need some help."

"Tank engines don't need help!" Thomas snapped. "We're Really Useful." And off he puffed.

Thomas pulled Annie and Clarabel and some empty trucks through the countryside. "Chickens to market, sheep to farm, children to school," he peeped.

Thomas' first job was to collect
the chickens. When he arrived,
the chickens were huddled
together on the track-side of the
Orchard. The farmhands put the
chickens into one of the trucks,
and off Thomas chugged towards
the valley to collect the sheep.

The Shepherd was waiting for Thomas, and the sheep were lined up next to the gate.

"Come on," peeped Thomas, to the sheep. "I'll take you to the Farm."

The sheep were soon loaded into the next empty truck. And off Thomas chuffed, to pick up the schoolchildren.

The platform at Maron Station was filled with schoolchildren. Thomas trundled in to the station with a truck full of chickens and a truck full of sheep – and Annie and Clarabel. He was very tired, his axles ached and his pistons were pounding. But the children's smiling faces made him feel happy. They climbed on board and he puffed away.

Thomas puffed up Gordon's Hill, past the Windmill, and through Henry's Tunnel.
It was a very long way to pull such a heavy load. "Chickens to market, sheep to farm, children to school," Thomas remembered.

The junction signal was red, and
Percy was waiting there, too.
Thomas ground to a halt beside
Percy. His axles were aching.
Percy could see how tired Thomas
looked and he was worried about
his friend.

"You look puffed out," said Percy.
"Would you like some help?"

"No, thank you," said Thomas.
"Really Useful Engines don't need
help." And he chuffed slowly away.

By the time Thomas reached the
station at the Market he was very
muddled. So muddled that he
asked his Foreman to unload the
sheep instead of the chickens.

Whilst the sheep were being
unloaded, Emily arrived.
She too, could see that Thomas
was tired.

"Would you like some help?"
Emily asked.

"No, thank you," puffed Thomas.
"Really Useful Engines don't
need help."

But Thomas did need help, he was
worn out. Once the sheep were
unloaded, Thomas puffed away.

Thomas continued puffing through the countryside. "Sheep to market, children to farm and chickens to school," he yawned sleepily.

When he reached Farmer McColl's, he told the children it was their stop. So, the children got off at Farmer McColl's and an exhausted Thomas puffed slowly away.

When he reached the School station, only the chickens were left. So, the chickens were unloaded.

Meanwhile, The Fat Controller was sitting in his office. He was getting lots of phone calls.

He took a call from the Farmers' Market. The sheep Thomas had unloaded had caused chaos!
They had knocked over all the stalls, and the fruit and vegetables were everywhere!

He took a call from Farmer McColl.
The children Thomas had delivered to the Farm were covered in straw and surrounded by pigs!

And, finally, he took a call from the Headmaster of the School, who had a classroom full of chickens!

Thomas had finally finished.
Edward, Percy and Gordon saw
how tired he was as he slowly
chuffed into the Shed.

Thomas was looking forward to
having a nice long sleep. Just as
he was about to close his eyes,
The Fat Controller arrived.
"Thomas, you have caused
confusion and delay," he said.

The Fat Controller explained what
had happened.

Thomas was VERY upset. He was VERY tired and now he had to do his jobs all over again.

"Don't worry, Thomas," reassured The Fat Controller. "All you need is some help."

"But Gordon said that a Really Useful Engine never needs help," peeped Thomas.

"Pah!" laughed Edward. "I'm always helping Gordon up the hill."

Gordon looked very embarrassed.

"Percy and Edward, you will help Thomas," said The Fat Controller.

So, Percy took the sheep from the Market back to the Farm.

Edward took the chickens from the School to the Market.

And Thomas collected the children
from the Farm.
"I'm sorry," Thomas puffed.
"I didn't mean to take you to the
wrong station."

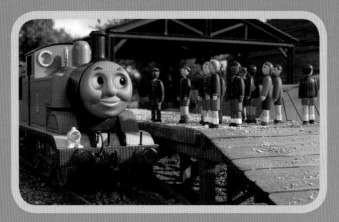

"We don't mind," said the children.
And they didn't. They'd had a grand
day out seeing the animals and
learning all about the Farm.

That night, when Thomas finally
got to sleep, he dreamt all about
sheep and chickens and children!